Terrific Toddlers

New Baby!

by Carol Zeavin, MSEd, MEd
and Rhona Silverbush, JD

illustrated by Jon Davis

Magination Press • Washington, DC • American Psychological Association

Magination Press is a registered trademark of the American Psychological Association. Order books at maginationpress.org,
or call 1-800-374-2721.

Book design by Gwen Grafft
Printed by Sonic Media Solutions, Inc., Medford, NY

Library of Congress Cataloging-in-Publication Data
Names: Zeavin, Carol, author. | Silverbush, Rhona, 1967- author. |
  Davis, Jon, 1969- illustrator.
Title: New Baby! / by Carol Zeavin, MSEd, MEd, and Rhona
  Silverbush, JD ; illustrated by Jon Davis.
Description: Washington, DC : Magination Press, [2020] | Series:
  Terrific toddlers | Summary: "When a new baby comes, toddlers
  often wonder what will happen"— Provided by publisher.
Identifiers: LCCN 2019043200 | ISBN 9781433832505 (hardcover)
Subjects: LCSH: Families—Juvenile literature. | Newborn
  infants—Juvenile literature. | Brothers and sisters—Juvenile
  literature.
Classification: LCC HQ744 .Z43 2020 | DDC 306.85—dc23
LC record available at https://lccn.loc.gov/2019043200

Manufactured in the United States of America
10 9 8 7 6 5 4 3 2

With gratitude to my inspiring teachers and mentors
at Bank Street, Rockefeller, and Barnard—CZ

Dedicated to the inspiration for this series
(you know who you are!), with infinite love—RS

For Laura and Greta—JD

More Terrific Toddlers

All Mine!

Boo-Boo!

Bye-Bye!

Potty!

Time to Go!

Sometimes a new baby comes.
Sometimes we worry about what will happen.

Kai's mommy has a very big belly.
There's a baby inside!
Kai doesn't know what to think.

"Pick up me, Mommy!" he cries.
"I see you're worried," Mommy says.

She cuddles him.
"You're my big boy—and my baby, too!
I will always be your mommy, and you will always be my baby."

The baby is almost born!
Kai doesn't know what will happen
when Mommy has the baby.

Daddy tells Kai, "Mommy and Daddy
will go to the hospital to have the baby.
Grandma and Grandpa will come stay with you.

Then we'll bring the baby home, and we will all be a family together."

The baby is home!

Kai doesn't know why the baby cries so much.
"Maybe the baby needs something," Daddy says.
"What do you think, Kai?"

"Baby diaper wet!" Kai says, and gets a diaper from the basket.
"Thank you, Kai," Daddy says.
He tells the baby, "Look — Kai is helping!"

Kai wants the baby to go away!
"No baby!" he yells. "No, no, NO!"

Mommy says, "I see you're angry.
That's okay. You can say, 'I'm angry!'

You can stomp, stomp, stomp your feet!

I love you, Kai, even when you're angry."

Kai has a mommy and a daddy, and a new baby.
Mommy is rocking the baby.
Daddy is showing Kai pictures...of Kai when he was a baby!

Then Kai says, "Mommy lap?"
"Yes, come," Mommy smiles.
"There's always room for
Kai in Mommy's lap.

You will always be our baby, and we will always be your mommy and daddy."

Note to Parents and Caregivers

"Congratulations—you're having a baby! We're so happy for you!"

Your toddler may not be so sure. Toddlers are just beginning to understand how they fit into their families and communities and don't know what this new person will mean. For toddlers, having a new sibling is a real shock—they may not even be sure you will still be their mommy and daddy! They are very confused about the little intruder—angry sometimes, genuinely in love other times. It's a complicated time.

Keep it simple. Answer their questions briefly and matter-of-factly. They are already overwhelmed, so try to limit how much you tell them. Try not to tell them too early that there's a baby coming—there's that much more time to build anxiety! When they notice Mommy's belly growing, simply explain that there's a baby growing inside (and use "toddler time" such as "when the leaves turn pretty colors" or "after Grandma visits" to answer questions about when the baby is coming out). And then wait until just a couple of weeks before the baby is due to give logistical details about what will happen around the birth—where they will be, and who will take care of them while the baby is being born.

Let them help. Toddlers love being helpful! Give them simple jobs, like fetching a blanket or a diaper. Including them in baby-related activities will help them feel that they are an important part of their newly-structured family.

Expect aggression. Attempts at hitting, biting, and grabbing things are normal. While protecting the baby, it's also important to validate and respect your toddler's anger by giving it an outlet. Having them stomp feet or make other appropriate physical expressions of anger has been shown to healthily reduce the upset, and shows you don't think the angry feelings are "bad." Labeling their feelings also helps (as Mommy does for Kai in the story when he's angry). Examples could include, "It's okay to be angry," or, "You're really mad!"

Expect regression. Toddlers with a new baby may wish to be a baby again, too, and they need to know that's OK with you. If they regress a bit—want a bottle, lose ground with potty training, want to be cuddled like a baby—indulge them for as long as they need. This reassurance will calm their fear of losing both you and their baby self, and it shows that you understand them.

Give them some one-on-one time. They used to have you all to themselves. They still need your whole-hearted and whole-bodied attention. Find games you can play together, an outing, a storytime...just Mommy and/or Daddy and toddler.

The most important thing you can do is to recognize and validate your toddler's fears and mixed feelings. Reassure them, as often as they show you they need, that they are still your baby, and that you will always be their mommy and daddy!

We love toddler pronunciation! And we know toddlers are not yet able to pronounce the 'R' sound in "diaper" or the 'L' sound in "lap." We just didn't want to annoy you with approximated spellings of most toddlers' best efforts ("die-pah," or maybe "die-pee;" "wap" or "yap"). So, don't worry if your toddler can't pronounce "diaper" or "lap" as well as Kai does—Kai can't, either!

Carol Zeavin holds master's degrees in education and special education from Bank Street College, and worked for eighteen years in homes and classrooms with toddlers. She was Head Teacher at both Rockefeller University's Child and Family Center and at the Barnard Toddler Development Center, and worked for Y.A.I. and Theracare. She is a professional violinist living in New York, NY.

Rhona Silverbush studied psychology and theater at Brandeis University and law at Boston College Law School. She represented refugees and has written and co-written several books, including a guide to acting Shakespeare. She currently coaches actors, writes, tutors, and consults for families of children and teens with learning differences and special needs. She lives in New York, NY.

Visit terrifictoddlersbookseries.com

🐦 @CarolRhona

📷 @TerrificToddlersBooks

Jon Davis is an award-winning illustrator of more than 80 books. He lives in England.

Visit jonsmind.com

🐦 @JonDavisIllust

📷 @JonDavisIllustration

Magination Press is the children's book imprint of the American Psychological Association. Through APA's publications, the association shares with the world mental health expertise and psychological knowledge. Magination Press books reach young readers and their parents and caregivers to make navigating life's challenges a little easier. It's the combined power of psychology and literature that makes a Magination Press book special.

Visit www.maginationpress.org

 @MaginationPress